Fiona's Dream Adventures
Written by: Martin Lundqvist

Fiona's Dream Adventures
First edition. 3 August 2021
Copyright © 2021 Martin Lundqvist.
Written by Martin Lundqvist

I0540095

Fiona and the Red Dragon

Fiona Orchard was sitting at home overlooking the skyline of Sydney's Eastern Suburbs. She felt bored. Her friend Rebecca had cancelled their tennis plans, so she had nothing to do. She approached her father Lars who was writing a book.

"Hi, daddy. Rebecca didn't want to play tennis with me. Do you want to play again?" Fiona said.

Lars got up, stretched his body, and grumbled. "No, I am too old to play twice in a day. Not everyone can be the best 7-year-old tennis player in Raleigh Park."

"Daddy, you are 43. How about becoming the best 43-year-old?" Fiona giggled.

"I am definitely in the top ten amongst the 43-year-olds," Lars replied truthfully, as there weren't that many people playing tennis in the suburb.

"So, what can I do to keep myself busy until mummy Ling-Ling comes home?" Fiona asked.

"You can read this book. It will open your mind," Lars replied and handed Fiona a book.

Fiona grabbed the book and squealed. It was one of the books her father had written, and he had read it to her many times in the past.

"Daddy. Haven't you already read this book for me many times?" Fiona asked.

"Yes, I have. But you have never read it yourself. Now that you are attending school, you need to practice your reading." Lars replied.

"Nah, I'd rather watch TV," Fiona said, got seated on the couch, and turned on the TV.

Fizz

Fiona watched in disappointment as the TV turned black. What had happened?

"Daddy! The TV is broken." Fiona yelled. Lars shook his head and replied, "No, the TV is not broken. I turned off all the power plugs in the apartment. You won't be able to use your devices, until you have read and recapped the plot of my book."

Fiona sighed. Her dad was both right and wrong. Reading was better for her than watching mind-numbing television shows. However, it was a shame that he scrimped and made her read his books, in-

2

stead of providing her with quality literature.

'Oh… If I was only old enough to visit the library,' Fiona thought. She realised that the closest library was two kilometres and several high traffic roads away. This was not a suitable hike for a seven-year-old.

'I'll ask mummy to take me when she gets home,' Fiona thought and went to her room to read her father's book to appease him.

As she turned the pages of the book, she had fond memories of listening to her father, and she got really sleepy. She put the book on her face, and she dozed off.

***

As Fiona woke up, she was in the world of Surrealia. 'Wow, so this is what Surrealia looks like.' Fiona thought as a book butterfly landed on her hand. The text on the book butterfly was, "Sometimes the best of intentions can have the worst of outcomes. Tread carefully."

'Hmm, that's odd. I wonder what that means?' Fiona thought and tried to decide what she wanted to see first. She wanted to see Morgor the Red Dragon. As terrifying

"No, the TV is not broken. I turned off all the power plugs in the apartment. You won't be able to use your devices, until you have read and recapped the plot of my book."

as that would be if this were reality, she was just dreaming, and she had always wanted to see a red dragon in person.

"Little girl. Who are you, and why are you here?"

Fiona turned towards the voice. It was an elderly flying fairy that spoke with an ethereal voice. 'Wow. That must be Finkerbelle the Mother Fairy.' Fiona thought and replied. "Hi, Finkerbelle. How are you today?"
"How do you know my name?" Finkerbelle asked in confusion.
"My father created you and these lands with the power of his imagination. I want to see Morgor the Red Dragon." Fiona chirped.
"I don't know what you are talking about, and you cannot see Morgor." Finkerbelle reprimanded. "Why is that? Have Diah Lubis already killed Morgor with her DKP-19 pistol?" Fiona asked.
"What are you talking about? Morgor isn't dead, and who is Diah Lubis?" Finkerbelle asked.
"Uhm, what year is it in Surrealia now?" Fiona asked.
"It's the 6th of May 2028. We have the same calendar as you do on Earth." Finkerbelle replied.

3

Finkerbelle's revelation made Fiona excited. She was in Surrealia, 160 years before Diah Lubis would arrive here. She was on her own adventure instead of reliving the adventures of her father. This was so exciting.

"I want to see Morgor at once," Fiona said. "It is too dangerous. Morgor is 30 metres long and he exhales fire." Finkerbelle objected.
"I don't care. This is my dream and I want to go on an adventure. You can't stop me." Fiona replied.

Finkerbelle responded by chanting nonsense and her face got red from the strenuous effort. Eventually, she replied. "As it would seem, my magical powers do not affect your dreaming powers. You are free to visit Morgor. He is in the Smoky Mountains to the east."
'Wow, this is so cool.' Fiona thought.

The mountain in the distance reminded her of Mount Ngauruhoe in New Zealand, which had been used to symbolise Mount Doom in the Lord of the Rings movies. Fiona had tried traversing the mountain with her parents the previous year, but it had been too far to walk for her tiny legs. However, she was in a dream now, so she could teleport to where she wanted. Fiona used her dream powers and teleported to Morgor's mountain.

Swoosh

***

"We must kill all the green dragons. Only

red dragons can remain in Surrealia."

At first, the dark hateful voice of Morgor speaking to his peers scared Fiona. Then she realised that this was her dream and that she had to put Morgor into place. To hate someone because of the colour of their skin was an outdated idea, and Fiona needed to teach him better ways.

"Don't be silly Morgor. You cannot hate someone because of the colour of their skin." Fiona shouted, but her voice felt weak in comparison to the thundering roar of Morgor.

Morgor and the other red dragons stared in bewilderment at Fiona with their glowing yellow eyes. One of the female dragons spoke. "What is a young human girl doing at our dragon meeting? You must be very brave."
"Or very foolish," Morgor growled.
"You are the fool, Morgor. Why do you hate green dragons so much?"   4

Fiona asked.

"I hate them because my father hated them, and he hated them because his father hated them, and so on. We have always hated the green dragons in my family." Morgor revealed.

"Death to the green dragons." The crowd chanted.

Fiona was almost blown away by the terrifying roars of the chanting dragons, and her ears were hurting from the loud noises.

Fiona gathered her willpower and exclaimed. "Enough. This is my dream, and you must stop hating others because of the colour of their skin."

"Why is that?" Morgor asked.

"Because racism is stupid. We humans used to kill each other because of our skin colours but we don't do that anymore. I have friends of all colours and creeds. I have white, yellow, brown and black friends." Fiona stated.

"Look who is the virtue signaller now." Morgor taunted.

"I am saying it as it is," Fiona replied.

"So, if racism is wrong, what is a good reason to hate others? We are dragons, we breathe fire. We thrive on hatred. Muahaha." Morgor said.

This was a tricky question. While hate was a

"Don't be silly Morgor. You cannot hate someone because of the colour of their skin."

basic emotion, and one couldn't deny basic emotions, Fiona didn't want to give the dragons a reason to hate.

"I know. We should hate the anthropomorphic ducks in Trumpyville. Their quacking is annoying, and their flesh is delicious." One of the dragons suggested.

"Aye, that's an excellent idea. Death to the ducks." Morgor roared.

Fiona sighed and remembered the text on the book butterfly. The worst-case scenario had come to pass. Her good intentions had united the dragons and the innocent humanlike ducks of Surrealia would suffer. She needed to fix this, but how?

The voice of her mother made the world of Surrealia fade into nothingness.

***

"So, did your father's book bore you so much?" Ling-Ling teased.

"No, it took me on a great adventure. Reading is so great for the mind." Fiona replied.

"Great. Tell your dad all about it. He loves to get inspiration for his books." Ling-Ling said.

Fiona nodded and rushed to Lars to 5

tell him about her adventure. At the end of her story, he said. "Wow, that's a good story. You'll become a better writer than I one day."

As Fiona had fulfilled her task, Lars kept his promise and turned on the power to the appliances in the apartment so Fiona could watch TV to dull her senses. 20 minutes later, Ling-Ling exclaimed. "Dinner is served. Come to the kitchen. We are having Peking Duck."

As Fiona looked at the roasted duck, she pitied the poor creature that had suffered and died for the family dinner. She realised that there would always be suffering and hatred in the world and the only thing she could affect was her actions and emotions. At least she could create a perfect world in her dreams. One day, she would imagine a fantasy world where everyone lived in bliss and harmony.

"So, did your father's book bore you so much?"
"No, it took me on a great adventure. Reading is so great for the mind."
"Great. Tell your dad all about it. He loves to get inspiration for his books."

Fiona and Ptolemaeus.

Fiona was watching a documentary together with her father, Lars, in her cosy apartment in Kensington. The theme of the documentary was the solar system, and much to her relief, Lars didn't spoil it by spouting his conspiracy theories. Instead, he was writing one of his novels, while following the documentary with one eye.

After watching the documentary, Fiona felt confused. Her father was never this quiet while watching serious programs. What was going on?

Fiona decided to find out, so she spoke. "You are very quiet today, daddy. Don't you have any comments on the content?"

"It was a good documentary with good visuals. I like space documentaries and many of my books take place in space." Lars replied.

"But do you believe in what the documentary said? What other perspectives are there?" Fiona said.

"Yes, I do. Because the prevailing alternative theory, the Flat Earth Theory, is utter hogwash." Lars replied.

"Why is that?" Fiona asked.

"Because all the other science in the world must be wrong for the flat earth theory to work. For instance, the supposed ice wall that stops people from falling off the earth would have a much larger circumference than Antarctica. Furthermore, the seasons and gravity itself don't work in that model." Lars explained.

"I understand. Is there no other theory that does make sense? Remember that you told me to always see things from several perspectives." Fiona asked.

Lars put away his laptop, stroke his chin for a while, and spoke, "Hmm, Ptolemy's geocentric model of the solar system was the accepted model for 1500 years. I guess it made a lot of sense."

"What is that model, daddy?" Fiona asked.

"In Ptolemy's model, the earth is round and the correct size. However, the sun is small and orbits the earth, while the planets are even smaller and orbits the sun." Lars replied.

"Wow. That makes more sense than the documentary we watched. Can you tell me more?" Fiona enthused.

"Uhm no. I need to go to work now. Have a look on the Internet if you want." Lars said, closed his laptop, and put on his soccer referee uniform.

Fiona felt a hint of disappointment

in her father's inability to explain the geocentric model. Fiona knew that there was no point in asking her mother Ling-Ling as she would only parrot the content of the textbooks. Thus, there was only one thing to do. She needed to use her dreaming abilities, meet with Ptolemy, and get him to explain his model.

Having made up her mind, Fiona went to her room, closed her eyes, and prepared to go on another fabulous adventure.

***

When Fiona opened her eyes, she found herself in the bustling city of Alexandria during antiquity. The Great Library of Alexandria stood as the centrepiece of the city, as the city was the centre of science.

'I'll find Ptolemy in there,' Fiona thought, and she walked in the direction of the library.

As she saw the cool monuments in the city honouring the Egyptian, Greek, and Roman gods, Fiona felt disappointed that she couldn't bring her parents into her dream. She had visited Alexandria with her parents, the previous year, but the monuments had been ruins and the city had been polluted. Not as cool as this.

"In Ptolemy's model, the earth is round and the correct size. However, the sun is small and orbits the earth, while the planets are even smaller and orbits the sun."

Fiona entered the library where she spotted a bearded man in robes tweaking a mechanical model of the solar system. He muttered as he made the cogs in the model go around, and the model made a squeaky sound.

Fiona hesitated for a bit. Her mummy had told her that she shouldn't approach strange-looking men, and Ptolemy in his long beard and robes looked eccentric. Fiona shook it off. While mummy Ling-Ling's advice was good for the real world, Fiona had nothing to fear in her dreams.

Fiona approached Ptolemy and spoke. "Hi, Ptolemy. Can you please explain how your geocentric model works?"

Ptolemy turned towards Fiona, studied her, and spoke: "Why are you calling me that strange name, girl, and where are you from? I have never seen a child like you before."

"Uhm, I am Fiona Orchard from Australia. What is your name?" Fiona replied.

"My name is Claudius Ptolemaeus, 9

and I am struggling with my model?" Ptolemaeus said.

"Oh, I see. Have you tried making the sun huge and have all the planets including earth orbit the sun?" Fiona suggested.

"Don't be silly. Everyone can see that the sun is a lot smaller than the earth. What I struggle with is getting this model to work without squeaking. Olive oil isn't good enough as a lubricant. I need something better." Ptolemaeus ranted.

'Oh, where can I get better oil?' Freya thought. She realised that she could summon petroleum-based lubricants since this was her dream.

"What about this oil?" Fiona said and handed Ptolemaeus a can of spray-on lubricant.

Ptolemaeus sprayed the oil on his hand, tasted it, and grimaced. "What is this oil? It tastes terrible." Fiona giggled and replied, "You are not meant to taste it, silly. Spray it on the cogs in your model."

Ptolemaeus muttered something inaudible, sprayed the cogs with the oil, turned the crank, smiled, and spoke. "Ah, music to my ears. The cogs have stopped squeaking. I am ready to show my model of the universe to the world!"

"I see. Can you explain the model to me?" Fiona asked.

"Since you helped me, I will. In my model, the Earth is in the centre of the universe. The sun is orbiting the earth at 1210 radii, while the other planets are tiny and orbit the sun. Furthermore, all the other stars are stuck at the edge of the universe at 20000

radii." Ptolemaeus replied.

"Cool. Can we fly closer to the sun on a Pegasus as Icarus did?" Fiona asked. Ptolemaeus laughed and replied. "I am afraid not. 1210 radii are the same as flying around the Earth 200 times. You are not going to do that on a horse."

Fiona nodded and replied. "I understand. How about going on a rocket?"

"What is a rocket?" Ptolemaeus asked.

"It is a big metal ship with fire coming out from the bottom. It is very fast. Come to the roof of the building and I'll show you." Fiona said and ran upstairs to the spaceship she had summoned to the top of the building with her dream powers.

***

"Three, two, one, ready for take-off!" Fiona chirped as she pressed the take-off button while she was in the spaceship with Ptolemaeus.

10

As she pressed the button, she had a realisation; starting a rocket on top of the most important library in history was a dumb idea. She didn't have the time to think about this, as the rocket pushed her back into her seat with a lot more force than the fastest of roller coasters.

"Don't be silly. Everyone can see that the sun is a lot smaller than the earth. What I struggle with is getting this model to work without squeaking."

mother's cooking and it smelled delicious.

"Wow, I never thought I would be able to visit space. A shame you burnt down the Great Library of Alexandria though." Ptolemaeus said.

"That's okay. It was bound to happen. It was a bit stupid to keep the originals of all the collected works of antiquity in a single place. Books are flammable." Fiona said.

"So, what do we do now?" Ptolemaeus said.

"Now that we have left Earth, we can find out whether the sun orbits the earth or vice versa. We can also find out whether the other planets are tiny or huge." Fiona said.

Unfortunately, Fiona couldn't get the answers she was looking for as a loud voice caused her dream to collapse unto itself.

***

"Fiona! Dinner is ready!" Mummy Ling-Ling shouted.

Fiona shook her head and smiled at the same time. She felt disappointed that she couldn't find out whether Ptolemaeus was right or wrong. However, she loved her

Fiona and the Halloween Alien.

Fiona Orchard was sitting at home and fiddling with her Halloween mask. For this year's trick or treating, she wanted to dress up like an alien, as she loved sci-fi movies and cute aliens are her favourite characters. The mask was very scary, and it would terrify everyone. This would be fun for a change, as she was normally a very cute girl.

There was, however, a tiny problem. Fiona's mummy Ling-Ling was not keen to let her go trick or treating as she was worried that it was unsafe.

Fiona thought that her mother was unfair, and decided to voice her concerns, "But mummy, why can't I go trick or treating in the neighbourhood. All the other children are going."
"It is too dangerous, my darling. I don't want you to knock at some bad person's door." Ling-Ling replied.
"But it's fun." Fiona objected.
"That doesn't matter. I bought you a bag of candy, which you can eat while hanging out with your friends afterwards." Ling-Ling replied.
"Mummy, don't take the fun out of Halloween," Fiona complained.
"I don't care. I am your mother; you should listen to me." Ling-Ling replied.

Hearing this, Fiona got frustrated, went to her room, and slammed the door behind her while crying.

As she was sulking angrily in her room, she heard that her father was coming home.

'Hmm, perhaps I can convince him to let me go trick or treating,' Fiona thought, approached Papa Lars, and spoke, "Hey papa. I am so happy to see you. How was your work?"
"It's nice to see you too, Fiona. What favours are you trying to solicit?" Lars replied and smirked kindly.
'Shoot, I must be too obvious,' Fiona thought and replied. "Umm.. Rebecca, Sandra, and I were thinking of tricking and treating since it is Halloween."
"Uh-huh. Your mother already said no, didn't she?" Lars replied.
"Sigh, yes," Fiona replied.
"Then you should listen to your mother," Lars replied.
"But why? She is silly and neurotic," Fiona whined.
"Well, trick or treating are not a suitable activity from a risk/benefit perspec-

tive," Lars replied. "What do you mean, papa?" Fiona asked. "The risk for a young girl knocking on someone's door is that she ends up in a lunatic's dungeon. The only perceivable benefit is a few dollars' worth of candy. Your mother and I agreed to eliminate that risk by buying enough candy for you and your friends." Lars explained. "But daddy, you are also killing the fun. Did you ever consider that?" Fiona whined. "Well, unfortunately, it is a parental responsibility to lessen risks for their children. Go to your room, Fiona. Let me know if you need a lift to your friend's house." Lars said and walked to the kitchen.

Hearing this, Fiona gave up. She grabbed her bag of candy and went to her room and grumbled. To calm her anger down, she ate the candy too quickly, felt a bit sick, and fell asleep.

***

When Fiona got back to her senses, she was trick or treating with Rebecca and Sandra.

'Wow, so I did convince my father to let me

> **"The risk for a young girl knocking on someone's door is that she ends up in a lunatic's dungeon. The only perceivable benefit is a few dollars' worth of candy. Your mother and I agreed to eliminate that risk by buying enough candy for you and your friends."**

trick or treat?' Fiona thought and considered whether she had left the apartment in an act of rebellion.

She felt a bit guilty for causing her parents to worry, but she got over it when she heard Rebecca chirp, "Wow, that house looks so cool. I bet they have the best candy!"

Fiona looked at the house. The proprietor had gone all-in with the decorations. Green snot was at the door handle, purple smoke oozed from the windows, and a spaceship was parked in the backyard.

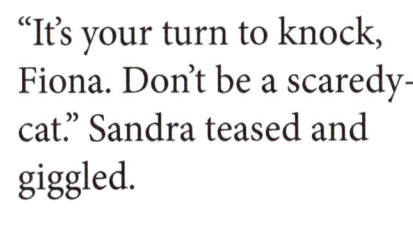

"It's your turn to knock, Fiona. Don't be a scaredy-cat." Sandra teased and giggled.

Fiona hesitated for a bit. She recalled that her mother had banned her from going, and her mother's worry was rubbing off on her. Then again, why would she allow fear to kill her fun? Fiona knocked on the door, and a slime-like creature that looked like a slimmer version of Jabba the Hutt opened the door.

"Gring, Grong, Grung." The alien said.

Fiona stared in a mix of terror and fascination at the hideous creature. Whoever lived here was certainly a Halloween enthusiast.

Fiona stuttered, "Trick or treat?"
"Ding, dong, dung," The alien replied.
"Uhm, can you speak English, please?" Fiona asked.
The alien squinted while looking at Fiona, grimaced, and replied. "Of course, I can speak English. But why would I speak English to my daughter? We must keep our Zung heritage as diplomats from the Wolf-359-star-system.

Fiona stared at the homeowner. What on earth was she talking about?

"Fiona, run. It is a monster!" Rebecca and Sandra shouted and fled the scene.

Before Fiona had the chance to run, the alien grabbed her and scolded her. "So, are you playing with human friends now? I am ashamed that you are not valuing your heritage. You are grounded, my young lady."
At first, Fiona was clueless why the alien thought she was her daughter, but then Fiona saw herself and the alien in the mirror. When Fiona wore her alien mask, she looked like the daughter of the slimy alien. "Let me go. I am a human." Fiona pleaded. "Don't say such a thing. Don't deny what you are!" The mother alien said, grunted, and burped out smelly purple ooze.

Having said this, the mother alien lifted Fiona over her shoulder, ignored Fiona's protests, and brought her downstairs to the dungeon.

"You'll stay grounded until you behave, young lady." The mother alien shouted and locked the door behind her.

Fiona cried as she was alone in the dungeon. She regretted that she didn't listen to her parents, although in all fairness, her parents had warned her about bad people. They had never mentioned smelly aliens with poor eyesight.

Oh yes, the eyesight. Perhaps this was a misunderstanding? Fiona pulled off her mask, started banging on the door, and shouted, "Let me out. I am a human. "Gring, Dong, Zung." The alien shouted and came rushing to the door.

As the alien opened the door she squinted towards Fiona and spoke. "Zung, why are you wearing a human mask. I told you that such a mask won't scare anyone on this planet."

"It's not a mask; it's my real face. I am a human." Fiona replied.

"I have had enough of your obsession with becoming human. I am taking you to our home planet so we can get help for your problems." The alien said, grabbed Fiona, and carried her like a sack of potatoes to the spaceship in her backyard.

Once they were on the spaceship, the alien strapped Fiona to a chair and started the engines. As the rocket propelled away from Earth, Fiona saw how her home became smaller and smaller.

"Mummy, I should have listened to you. I am sorry…" Fiona sobbed and sobbed and sobbed. Awwww!

***

"Fiona. Your friends are here."

Fiona woke up with a twist and she felt relieved to find out that she had been dreaming. What a nightmare!

Fiona looked at her alien mask that was on the floor. She would never wear that one again. She came to the door to greet her friends Rebecca and Sandra.

"Hi, guys. How was the trick or treat?" Fiona asked.

The alien squinted while looking at Fiona, grimaced, and replied. "Of course, I can speak English. But why would I speak English to my daughter? We must keep our Zung heritage as diplomats from the Wolf-359-star-system.

"It wasn't very good. A lot of people didn't answer the doors, and most didn't have any candy to give us." Sandra replied.

"No candy?" Fiona asked.

"Yes, trick or treat are not as common here as it is in the American movies," Rebecca replied.

"Oh, but I have a lot of candy. Let's eat it and watch princess movies." Fiona chirped.

"Yes. We will have so much fun," Sandra exclaimed.

Having said this, the girls got seated by the TV to watch princess movies.

They had a great time and enjoyed the candy Fiona's parents had given to her to alleviate the risk of her ending up in a dungeon.

Fiona and the Einstein Encounter

Fiona was looking at her first school report card from Kensington Public School. Her dreaming abilities didn't transform into good grades, and with an average of Cs in most of her school subjects, she was just a regular Year 3 student.

To daddy Lars, this was an acceptable outcome, but to mummy Ling-Ling, it wasn't. For Ling-Ling, like many other Asian parents, her child needed to achieve what she had never achieved herself, to be the top in her class.

Fiona went home with a sad look on her face. She feared telling her mother about her grades, but she wanted to get it done so she could enjoy the rest of the summer holiday in peace. Yet, the feeling of disappointment was hard to take, and she started crying on her way home.

Lars met her in the park outside of their apartment. He gave her a concerned look and said: "Why are you crying, Fiona. Did something bad happen in school?"
"I feel so stupid…" Fiona sobbed.
"Why do you say that?" Lars replied in disapproval.
"My grades… I got Cs in average." Fiona replied.
"Getting a C does not make you stupid, it is average. So, don't feel that way." Lars replied.
"But mummy will be upset with me." Fiona sobbed again.
"Yes, but you are not living your life to please mummy, right?" Lars said.

"I guess you're right, daddy," Fiona replied. "Good. Just be a good girl who lives a good life and doesn't harm anyone, and I couldn't be prouder of you." Lars said, picked her up, and then kissed her cheek.

Fiona felt comforted by her father's words and his embrace. Lars was correct. If she was of average intelligence and she hadn't harmed anyone with her actions, then what was there to be sad about?

"So, will you speak to mummy for me?" Fiona asked.
"No, but I am telling you this. Although Ling-Ling will voice her disappointment with you, she still loves you. Some days aren't going to be amazing, that's life. But in a few days, we are going to Gold Coast so you can visit all the theme parks. That

will be fun, won't it?" Lars said
"Yes!" Fiona chirped.
"So, do you want to come exercising with daddy?" Lars asked.
"No, I would rather go home and take a nap. I couldn't sleep last night because I was so nervous about my grades." Fiona admitted.
"Okay, I'll take you home before I head out," Lars replied and carried little Fiona back to their apartment.

As they got home, Lars tucked her in bed and left the apartment quietly.

'Oh, I wish this day could be over,' Fiona thought and fell asleep, exhausted from her night of undue worries.

***

As Fiona woke up, she was in a historical European city, which she didn't recognise. A lot of people were riding horse carts, while a few were driving very old-looking cars.

She walked up to a woman and spoke, "Hi, I am Fiona, and I am lost. Where and when am I?"
The woman chuckled and replied, "You are lucky that this is a dream, otherwise I would find you crazy for asking. You are in the

"The theory of Relativity. I got it all figured out, but I am lacking my breakthrough formula."
"Ah, do you mean like E=MC2?"

Swiss city of Bern, and the year is 1905."

The woman's reply didn't make sense to Fiona. Why was she dreaming about being in Switzerland in the year 1905? What was going on?

'Wow, that must be Albert Einstein.' Fiona thought when she saw an eccentric man who was scribbling in a notebook while sitting under a tree. Fiona decided to talk to Einstein. He was the most intelligent man in human history, and he could teach her to be smart as well.

"Hi, Professor Einstein." Fiona chirped.
"Oh hi, little girl. I am not a professor. I am a bored patent clerk who is working on a theory." Einstein said.
"Okay, it looks like you are scribbling nonsense to me. What is your theory called?" Fiona asked.
"The theory of Relativity. I got it all figured out, but I am lacking my breakthrough formula." Einstein replied.
"Ah, do you mean like E=MC2?" Fiona asked.

Einstein looked at Fiona in amazement, scribbled for a bit and exclaimed, "Wow! You've helped me with the missing calculation of my formula chain.

You must be so smart!"

"Uhm, I am just an average student. I worry that my mum will feel disappointed when she hears about my grades." Fiona admitted. Einstein smiled at Fiona and replied, "Don't worry. Everybody is a genius. But if you judge a fish by its ability to climb a tree, it will live its whole life believing that it is stupid."

"So are you saying that I have great abilities?" Fiona asked.

"Yes. Not everyone can meet historical figures with the power of their minds." Einstein replied.

"Thank you, Einstein!" Fiona said happily.

"Please call me Albert," Einstein replied and winked.

Hearing Einstein's encouraging words, Fiona felt good again. No matter what her mother would say about her grades, she was happy with the way she was, and that was the most important thing in life.

"Thank you, Albert. Before I leave, can you tell me what your theories say?" Fiona said. "According to my theories, we can get limitless energy, powerful weapons, and time travels. Everyone is saying that I am crazy, but one day my dreams will come true." Einstein replied.

Fiona sighed. She knew that the only thing that had come from Einstein's theories was the invention of nuclear weapons. In the year 2027, limitless energy and time travel were still distant dreams. Yet, why would she destroy the spirits of the gentle eccentric man who had helped her?

"Thank you, Albert. It is time for me to wake up now," Fiona said and woke up in her room.

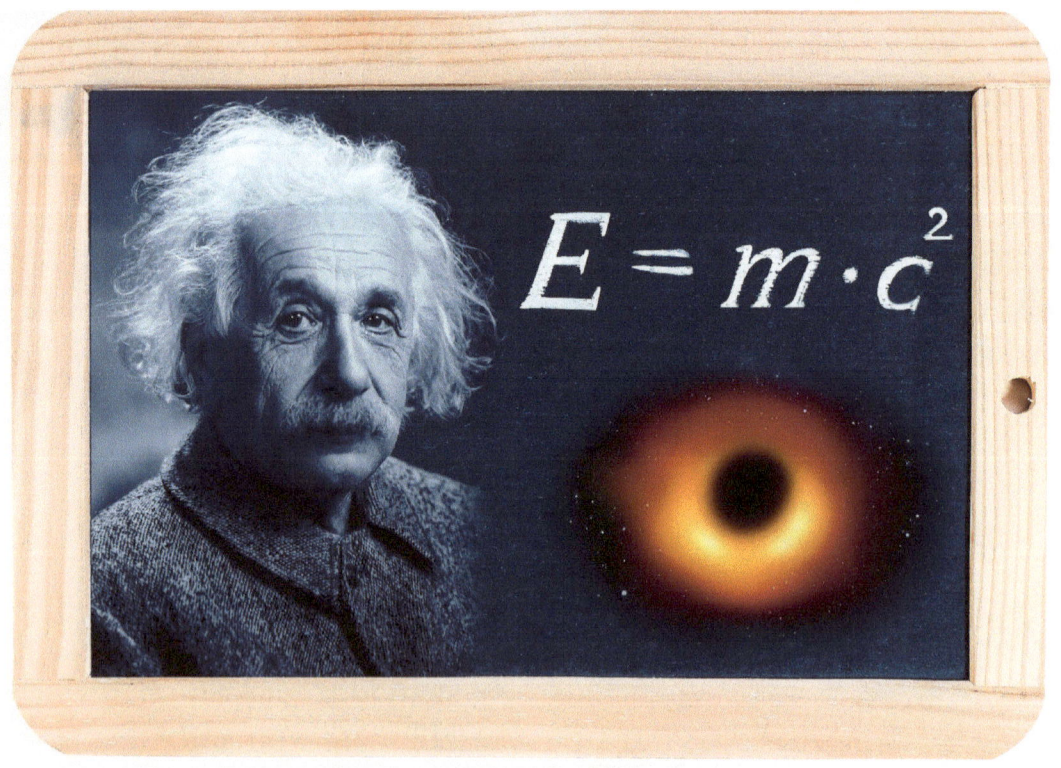

***

Fiona felt nervous as she approached the dinner table. Her mum hadn't mentioned her grades but she feared that the topic would come up. As she approached the dinner table, she saw a cake with the following text on the frosting. 'Congratulations to our favourite daughter for having better grades than half of her class.'

Fiona squealed in excitement, looked at Ling-Ling, and spoke, "Ha! So, you are not disappointed with my lack of good grades?" Ling-Ling faked a smile and replied, "I am, but I don't want you to feel like a failure. I love you, no matter what your grades are, and I want you to find motivation to do well in whatever you do."
"Thank you mummy," Fiona replied.
"So, what are we waiting for, let's eat this

"Don't worry. Everybody is a genius. But if you judge a fish by its ability to climb a tree, it will live its whole life believing that it is stupid."

cake!" Lars exclaimed.
"Not so fast, my dear. First, we need to eat dinner. I made a chicken salad to balance out the unhealthy cake." Ling-Ling replied and smiled.

After Ling-Ling said this, the family had a great night together. Fiona felt relieved that her mediocre grades hadn't caused any grief, and she felt motivated to try harder next term. After all, if she studied harder to quench her thirst for knowledge, she would feel much more motivated than if she studied hard to avoid punishment.

The chicken salad and the cake were yummy, and in a few days, she would go to Gold Coast and ride all the rollercoasters.

Weeeee!

Fiona and the Elven King

Fiona was bushwalking with her daddy when she saw something that fascinated and terrified her. She saw an eagle that dropped from the sky and caught a rabbit with an impressive swoop. While the eagle's graceful movements were a force of nature, she felt sad for the rabbit's demise. Rabbits were so cute and fluffy. Playing with her friend Jasmine's pet bunny had given her a lot of fun throughout the years. Fiona needed to stop the eagle!

"Daddy, we must stop the eagle from killing the rabbit," Fiona exclaimed.
"Killing? The eagle is inviting the rabbit for tea and cookies. Flying there is the quickest way." Lars teased.

Her daddy's comment made Fiona upset. She pushed him and exclaimed, "Don't make fun of me, daddy. The eagle is going to kill the rabbit. We must stop it."
"Sorry kiddo, but the eagle and the rabbit are over there, and we are here. We don't have wings. How do you suggest that we stop the eagle?" Lars said and chuckled.
"I wish we had a gun. Then we could shoot the eagle for being so mean." Fiona suggested.
"Well, apart from that shot being impossible, we would also kill the rabbit if we shot the eagle. A fall from that altitude wouldn't be survivable. Besides, the eagle killing the rabbit is the natural chain of events." Lars explained.
"I guess you are right. Can we become vegans, so our lifestyles don't harm innocent animals?" Fiona asked.

"Nope. Abstaining from meat is not a sacrifice I am willing to make to appease your whims and wishes. Besides, even a vegan lifestyle causes other animals to suffer." Lars replied.
"No! Vegans don't consume animal products. They are kind to the environment." Fiona objected.
"Yet, even if you were to become a vegan, you would want mobile phones, laptops, and the latest fashion items. The production of these objects damages the environment and causes suffering to animals." Lars replied.

Her daddy's words upset Fiona. She didn't like how he had shot down her idea of becoming a vegan without considering a compromise. Then again, Lars was old and set in his ways.

"So, is there a way to create a world without suffering?" Fiona asked.

"The fictional planet of Elvonia that I created was close to a paradise before Rangda and her Xenos invaded the planet. You can ask King Mellron about his world in your next dream," Lars suggested.

"Okay, daddy," Fiona replied and looked away.

They kept walking for another two hours, but Fiona couldn't enjoy the landscapes and the fresh air in Royal National Park. Witnessing the cruelty of nature had made her upset, and she loathed that such a cute creature had to suffer.

Eventually, they reached their car, and started the drive home. After riding the car for a while, Fiona got tired from her sulking and fell asleep.

***

When Fiona woke up, she was in a tranquil forest where everything glimmered with a magical light. It was the most beautiful forest she had ever seen, and the soothing sound of water from a nearby creek made her sleepy. 'I am not going to fall asleep; I want to

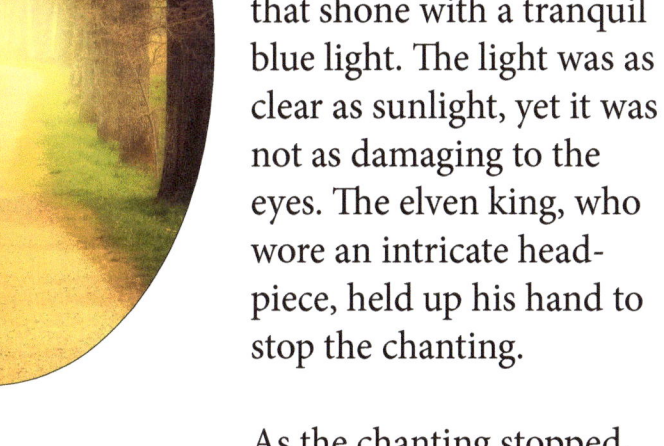

"The fictional planet of Elvonia that I created was close to a paradise before Rangda and her Xenos invaded the planet. You can ask King Mellron about his world in your next dream,"

explore this magical place.' Fiona thought and forced herself to stay awake. She walked towards the sound of the water and reached an ancient temple. Next to the temple, there was a waterfall, which shimmered in a mixture of blue and red from the soon-to-set sun. She heard chanting in a mysterious language from the inner sanctum of the temple.

Fiona walked inside the temple to investigate. She liked this dream, and she couldn't wait to see where it would lead her.

"Dawski Tor, Dawski Dage, Dawski Uung. Miua Elvonia. (For the past, for the present, for the future, my Elvonia.)"

Fiona saw a group of Elves that were chanting in front of a majestic blue crystal that shone with a tranquil blue light. The light was as clear as sunlight, yet it was not as damaging to the eyes. The elven king, who wore an intricate headpiece, held up his hand to stop the chanting.

As the chanting stopped, the king stepped down from the altar, and spoke, "Greetings. I am King Mellron. What is a human girl doing on Elvonia?"

"Hi, King Mellron. My name is Fio- 21

na, and I am here to learn about your ways. My father said that this planet is a paradise. The perfect world, where no one suffers?" Fiona asked.

"Oh yes, your father is correct. I wish that humanity could live the same way. Then again, you are not as aligned to the True Maker as we elves are." Mellron explained.

"Who is the True Maker?" Fiona asked.

"The True Maker is the creator of the universe. She is ever-present in Elvonia through the benevolent force of the Zeto Crystals. All creatures on this planet are living in harmony until the end of their lifespans when they pass on without fear in their hearts." Mellron claimed.

"So, are all the animal's herbivores?" Fiona asked.

"No. The carnivores have a crucial role on this planet. Whenever a plant-eater reaches the end of its lifespan, that animal offers itself on the altar of the afterlife. Carnivores surround that altar, and they kill the sick animals, causing as little pain as possible. As the carnivores eat the sick animals, they spread its nutrients through their droppings and thus causing an endless cycle of life." Mellron explained.

"Wow, that's so great. Why isn't the ecosystem working like that on earth?" Fiona asked.

"Earth wasn't created to be a paradise. It has another important purpose, which only the True Maker knows about." Mellron explained.

Fiona nodded but didn't say anything.

"Hey daddy, can I play with the human?" A young elven boy chirped.

Mellron gave the boy a strict look and re-

plied. "No, Adaron, you cannot. We need to chant Miua Elvonia 98 more times before we eat supper, and we are late as Fiona interrupted us."

"Hold on. This is my dream and I want Adaron to show me around." Fiona demanded.

Mellron gave Fiona a resigned look, sighed, and replied, "Okay, Fiona with the dreaming powers. This is my kingdom, but it is your dream. Make sure that my son behaves and are home in time for supper."

"I promise. Come Adaron, let's go on an adventure." Fiona chirped and the two children sprinted out from the temple so they could go on an adventure before Adaron needed to be home for dinner.

As they got out of the temple, Fiona saw a Pegasus. She had never seen a flying horse before, and this made her excited.

"Wow, a winged horse. Can we fly it?" Fiona chirped.

"I guess. Mitchki, come here." Adaron called, and the Pegasus approached them.

Fiona and Adaron got on the winged horse, and Fiona chirped with excitement. "Weeee. What is the best place to visit?"

"I don't know. You should decide." Adaron replied.

"Let's head for that cliff then," Fiona said and steered the horse to a nearby cliffside, which had an apple tree with blue apples on the top.

As they landed, Fiona got off the horse and grabbed a few apples from the apple tree. "Let's eat some apples and enjoy the sunset,"

"I don't have free will. Every day is a repetition of the previous day. Your arrival is the most exciting thing that has ever happened to me. I wish I was on Earth, where people and animals have free will."

Fiona said and the children got seated. "It's beautiful up here. Do you come here often?" Fiona asked while chewing the blue apple that tasted like a hybrid between plums and apples. "No, never…" Adaron replied. "Why not? It's so close to your home. Where do you like to go?" Fiona asked. "I… I don't know." Adaron stuttered. "What's the matter?" Fiona asked. "I don't have free will. Every day is a repetition of the previous day. Your arrival is the most exciting thing that has ever happened to me. I wish I was on Earth, where people and animals have free will." Adaron exclaimed.

Fiona looked at Adaron and reflected on what he had said. On the surface, Elvonia

seemed like a paradise. However, the way Adaron described life here, it seemed like an endless slog. Paradise wasn't what she wanted, she wanted life on earth with its joys and sorrows.

"Uhm, my father will be upset that I am late for dinner. This has never happened before." Adaron mumbled.
"Don't worry. This is a dream." Fiona said, hugged Adaron, closed her eyes, and woke up in the car as it parked at their Kensington home.

***

"Fiona, why are you running?" Lars asked as she ran out of the car.
"I need to say something to mummy, see you soon." Fiona chirped and rushed to the elevator.

As she entered her apartment, she rushed to hug her mother and chirped. "Thank you, mother. I am so glad that your God Jesus gave us free will."

"I am glad to hear that, but please tell me what happened," Ling-Ling replied.
"So, I saw an eagle kill a rabbit when I was bushwalking with daddy. I felt sad, and I dreamt about the perfect world where bad things never happened. I arrived at Elvonia, and it seemed perfect until a boy told me that the reason nothing bad happened was that their deity didn't grant them free will. That's why I am happy to be a human on earth."
"Wow, my little darling. You have the most vivid dreams. I have some good news. I have baked an apple pie for you. You deserve it after your long walk." Ling-Ling said and smiled.
"Mummy, you're the best." Fiona chirped and she helped herself to Ling-Ling's delicious apple pie.

Fuiba grabbed a plate and went to the balcony to watch the sunset, happy to know that it was her choice to do so.

I arrived at Elvonia, and it seemed perfect until a boy told me that the reason nothing bad happened was that their deity didn't grant them free will. That's why I am happy to be a human on earth."

Fiona and the Purest Diamond.

Fiona was watching mummy Ling-Ling who was admiring her jewellery collection. While Ling-Ling's diamonds were far from the largest in the world, she seemed mesmerised when she looked at the transparent stones. Fiona couldn't understand her mummy's fascination or why she kept the rocks in the safe. The week before, her dad had bought similar stones to Fiona in the toy store for a dime and a nickel.

"Hey mummy, why are you locking your stones away in a safe instead of playing with them?" Fiona asked.
"Oh, that's because I worry that I will lose them if I take them out and play with them. They are secure if I keep them in a safe." Ling-Ling replied.
"But what's the point of buying expensive toys if you can't play with them?" Fiona asked.
"The point of having these jewelleries is knowing that I own them and that I can look at them whenever I want." Ling-Ling replied.

Fiona shook her head. She couldn't understand her mother's infatuation with sparkly stones, since she never took them out to play. She decided to discuss the topic with Daddy Lars.

Lars was watching a corny comedy show when Fiona approached him. He smiled at her and spoke, "Hi Fiona. Did you get bored of mummy's gemstones already?"
"Yes, I don't know why she has pieces of jewellery if she never uses them. Are they

good as investments?" Fiona asked.
"Since when do you care about investments?" Lars asked.
"I listened to you and Uncle Geoffrey discussing investments, the other day. I met Warren Buffet in my dreams that night. I want to be as good at investing as he was, or at least, I want to be better than you and Geoffrey are." Fiona revealed.

Hearing this, Lars chuckled. It was a good thing that Fiona had an achievable dream, to back up her unrealistic one. Being better than him or Geoffrey when it came to investing, was a low bar to beat!

"Rare gemstones can sell for a fortune at auctions. The one's your mother buys lose 80 per cent of their value, as soon they leave the store." Lars revealed.

"Why is that daddy?" Fiona asked. "Because if something is mega rare, the rich will pay a fortune for it, because they can. The gemstones mummy buys are common stones, which are propped up by market manipulation and advertising." Lars explained.

"Okay. Thanks for the advice. Now I know that I need to find a rare diamond and sell it." Fiona said and left.

"Good luck, my dear," Lars said, chuckled and turned his attention back to the comedy show.

Hearing this, Lars chuckled. It was a good thing that Fiona had an achievable dream, to back up her unrealistic one. Being better than him or Geoffrey when it came to investing, was a low bar to beat!

'Oh, I'll show him.' Fiona thought and went to her room to visit the place where everything was possible; her dreams.

***

When Fiona opened her eyes, camera flashes were blinding her. Where had her dreams taken her?

"Behold. Fiona Orchard, the proprietor of the Orchard Diamond, the world's largest and purest diamond.

Fiona looked at the auctioneer who stood on the other side of the large diamond. She didn't get what the big deal was. To her, it looked like a large piece of prismatic glass.

'Hmm, maybe it has some magical properties,' Fiona thought. She decided to chant the verse she had heard on Elvonia during a previous adventure, "Dawski Tor, Dawski Dage, Dawski Uung, Miua Elvonia (For the past, for the present, for the future, my Elvonia.)"

The chanting did not affect the diamond, and now everyone was looking at her. How awkward!

"Uhm, it is a very beautiful diamond. Please bid for it." Fiona said in embarrassment.

"You heard the young lady. Did I hear $10million?" The auctioneer chanted.

"Aye!" a man replied.

"$15million?" The auctioneer continued.

"Here!" A woman replied.

Hearing how the audience members tried to outbid each other, Fiona smiled and dreamed about how life would be once the money was hers.

"Don't be greedy, you'll be happier if you only keep enough money to live 27 an honest life."

Fiona turned to the voice. It belonged to Finkerbelle, the mother fairy. Finkerbelle had warned Fiona about seeing the red dragons during an earlier adventure. Fiona hadn't listened to Finkerbelle on that occasion, and she had caused a lot of harm by inadvertently uniting the dragons against the rest of Surrealia's inhabitants.

"Okay. I'll listen to you this time. What do you want me to do?" Fiona asked.
"Keep a million for yourself and use the remaining money to open a school for disadvantaged children overseas," Finkerbelle instructed.
"Deal," Fiona replied, and her dream teleported her to another location.

***

"Look who is here, Nona Orchard."

As Fiona opened her eyes, she was at a school building somewhere in Asia. A bunch of children were playing soccer, and they were having a great time. They stopped playing and cheered when they saw her.

"What happened?" Fiona asked Finkerbelle. "It is the power of sharing. You sacrificed your needless luxury so all these children could stop working in the textile factory. Your contribution gave them an education and a good childhood like you have."
"So, all these good things happened because I gave up ownership of that clear rock?" Fiona asked. "Yes," Finkerbelle said and smiled.

Fiona smiled. What a wonderful dream, which had taught her one thing. That no diamonds in the world can outshine a pure heart.

Fiona smiled. What a wonderful dream, which had taught her one thing. That no diamonds in the world can outshine a pure heart.

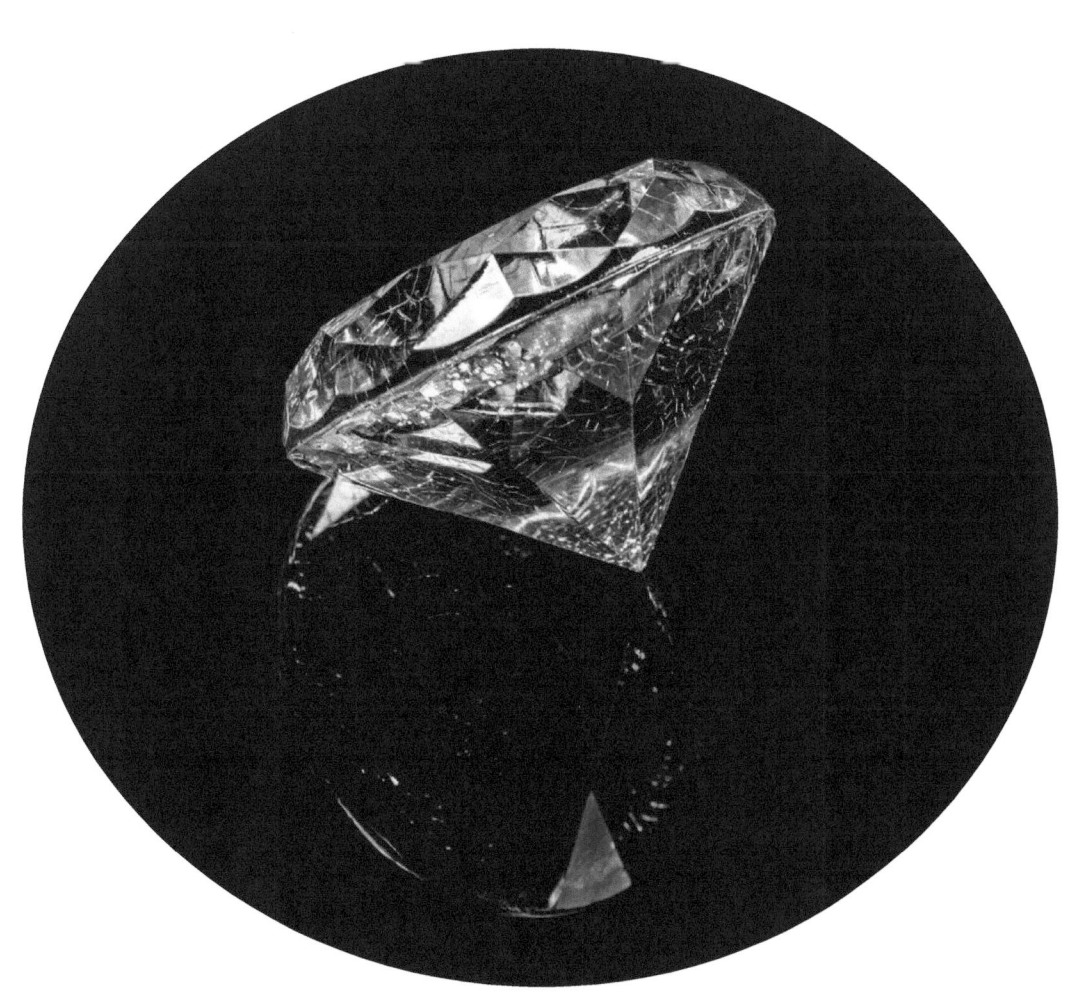

Fiona and the Vikings.

Fiona was watching a documentary about Vikings with her father, and she started to get irritated at the old man. It seemed like Lars was proud of sharing a heritage with the violence-prone Norsemen who terrorized Europe in the 9th century. Why were their raids a good thing, and why was her father so fascinated by them? Fiona decided to find out.

"Hey, daddy. Why are you so fascinated by the Vikings? They seem mean and stupid to me." Fiona asked.

"Well, my girl. The Viking Age is the most famous times of our people, and although they seem brutish and barbaric by today's standards, so was everyone else. The Vikings were just better at it." Lars said and chuckled.

"The Vikings were not my people. I look more Indonesian." Fiona objected.

"Looks got nothing to do with it. You have my blood in your veins. Besides, I am sure some Indonesian tribes did something you don't like at some point in time. What will you be then?" Lars teased.

"If that's the case, then I am just a human with no nationality," Fiona argued.

"Very well, non-descript human. I'll let you choose the next TV show." Lars joked.

"That's okay. But I must ask you. Why did they believe in going to heaven if they died in combat? That's so silly!" Fiona said.

"Hmm, why do you believe in going to heaven if you live a good life?" Lars asked.

"Uhm, because Jesus rewards the righteous?" Fiona replied with doubt in her voice.

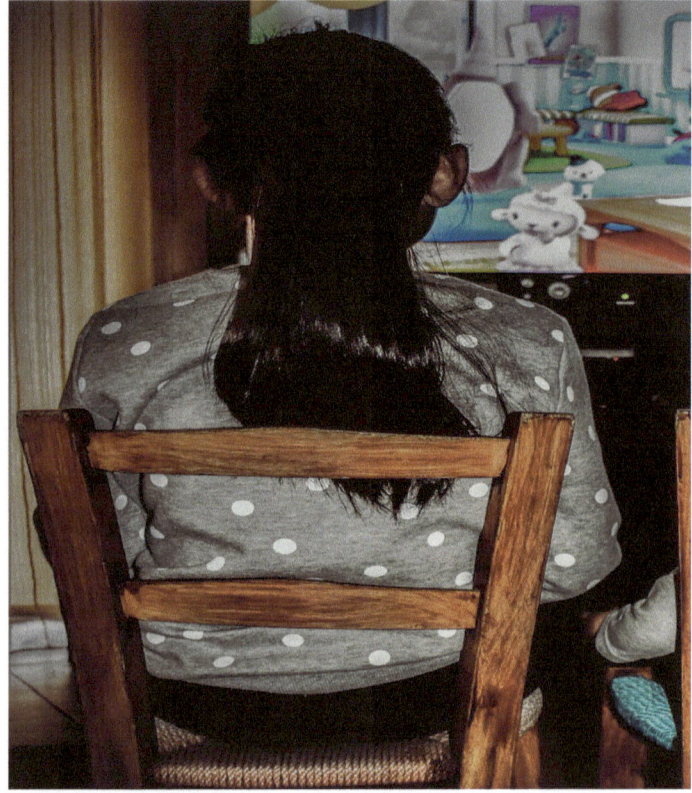

"Nah, that's not it. You believe it because Ling-Ling told you to believe in it during your formative years. You can tell a child between the ages 3-9 any religious mumbo jumbo, and they will carry on believing it into their adulthood." Lars explained.

"So, what do you believe in, daddy?" Fiona asked.

"I was not taught any religious doctrine in my formative years, so I don't believe in any of them. In any case, no religious belief is stranger or more absurd than any other belief, so you should keep an open mind." Lars replied.

Lars's answers annoyed Fiona. If he was correct, living a good life wouldn't bring any rewards in the end as there was no heaven.

But was living a good life in itself a

30

reward?

In any case, it was pointless pushing her mother's faith unto her father; there were much better ways to enjoy a Saturday afternoon. Such as taking a nap!

"Okay. I am not going to argue with you. I'll have my afternoon nap now." Fiona said.
"Wise choice. I'd nap more if I had as interesting dreams as you have, my dear," Lars replied and kissed Fiona on her forehead.

Fiona went to her bed and smiled at the book that was on her nightstand table. Through trial and error, she had found a book that was even better than her father's books at making her sleepy. Reading a few pages of The Bible: King James Version, written in 1611, was the best way to fall asleep!

***

'Wow, that was quick.' Fiona thought when she opened her eyes.

Fiona was at Glumslövs backar in the south of Sweden, and it was a beautiful summer

"Well, my girl. The Viking Age is the most famous times of our people, and although they seem brutish and barbaric by today's standards, so was everyone else. The Vikings were just better at it."

day. But when was it? Fiona realised that it wasn't present time when a dirty woman in white rags came running towards her. "Stranger, please help me. Today is Chieftain Bjorn Bredyxa's funeral." The woman stated.
"Why is that a problem?" Fiona asked.
"Because I, Sigrid Stormorm, am his bride for the afterlife," Sigrid replied.
"What does that title mean?" Fiona asked.
"It means that I need to be burnt together with his corpse on his ship," Sigrid replied.
"Oh no, that's terrible," Fiona said.

"It is. I don't want to be with Bjorn in the afterlife, I want to be with Knut." Sigrid revealed.

Fiona reflected on Sigrid's statement. It seemed absurd that Sigrid's main concern was that she would be sacrificed to the wrong chieftain.

Fiona knew one thing; it was time to spread her father's atheism doctrine to the Vikings. It would be difficult to convince them about the value of mercy, so it would be easier to convince them that it was idiotic to murder their slaves and burn their ship!

"Take me to your village, and I'll deal with the Vikings," Fiona said.

"What can you do? You are just a girl, and you are not even from here?" Sigrid replied.

"My father is from here, and I have powers that can change everything in this world," Fiona stated.

"You're crazy!" Sigrid said.

"No, I am not. Follow me." Fiona said and the duo walked back to the village.

***

"So, you have returned. Because of your insolence, you'll no longer go to Valhalla with our master. You'll go to hell which is your destiny as a slave. Muahaha!" A Viking raider taunted as Fiona and Sigrid approached the chieftain's funeral.

Fiona looked at the fearsome Norsemen. They had painted themselves with animal blood, and they were ready for their favourite activity, murder. She was lucky that this was her dream, otherwise, she would feel terrified.

"No. No one is going to die here today, and you are not going to burn that ship." Fiona commanded.

"And why is that?" The Viking taunted.

"Because it is all made up mumbo jumbo. Bjorn Bredyxa is dead, and nothing you do will change his afterlife." Fiona explained.

"That's rich coming from a Christian. We might kill you as well." The Viking roared.

Fiona noticed the crucifix that hung around her neck. This wasn't the best accessory to

wear while trying to promote the advantages of atheism, but she had to deal with it. "My cross is because my mum taught me Christianity during my formative years. That is what religion is, ideas taught during childhood. Your religion causes you to bury your treasures, and then you go overseas to rob more treasures. It's an endless vicious cycle, which has to end." Fiona explained.

The Vikings looked at Fiona in amazement. They had never imagined that a small girl would be brave enough to face them.

An older Viking approached Fiona and spoke, "So, what should we do instead?"

"You should dig up Bjorn's treasures and invest in your village, instead of robbing people overseas," Fiona replied.

Hearing this, the older Viking got moved by emotions, sprung to tears, and shouted, "Hilda. I finally get to spend a summer with you and my grandchildren. No more meaningless violence."

As Fiona watched the Vikings drop their weapons to hug their wives and children, she felt moved. It seemed that their religion had stopped them from embracing their humanity.

The joy was short-lived, as another group of Vikings came rushing with drawn swords.

'Time to wake up.' Fiona thought, closed her eyes, and opened them again, to wake up in her bedroom.

***

When Fiona opened her eyes, her dad stood by her bed. He smiled at her and spoke. "Hi, Fiona. I hope you had a good nap. I am sorry for pushing my atheism onto you."
"Did mummy make you say that?" Fiona

teased.
"Yes," Lars admitted.

"My cross is because my mum taught me Christianity during my formative years. That is what religion is, ideas taught during childhood. Your religion causes you to bury your treasures, and then you go overseas to rob more treasures. It's an endless vicious cycle, which has to end."

Viking tribe stop embracing violence."
"Oh, really? Did it work?" Lars asked.
'For about 5 minutes,' Fiona thought but instead she replied, "Yes, it went well."
"That's great. Let's have dinner. I made chicken salad with couscous for us." Lars said.
"Weeeee, yummy! Thank you, dad." Fiona chirped.

"Don't worry about it," Fiona replied happily.

Lars nodded and was about to leave when Fiona chirped. "Hey dad, I used your atheism arguments to make a

Having said this, Fiona hugged her dad and rushed to the kitchen to enjoy a well-deserved dinner.

Fiona and the Healthy Lollies.

It was raining outside, and Fiona was reading a book to improve on her vocabulary. While the TV and cartoons were more enticing, her father Lars had offered her $20 for reading one of his books and summarizing the plot. Reading was good for her, and it was nice to show some interest in her father's hobbies.

As she read the book, which followed her father's alter ego, she wondered why her father hadn't come up with a nicer depiction of himself. The Lars she knew wouldn't travel the world to murder people and steal magical artefacts, so why had he written that story? Fiona decided to ask.

She went to the living room where Lars was drinking beer and watching soccer. He wasn't following his own advice about reading to improve one's vocabulary. Yet at least he wasn't arguing about conspiracy theories online, so things could be worse.

"Uhm, daddy. I have a question?" Fiona asked.
"Yes, love. How can daddy help you?" Lars replied.
"So, in the book that you forced me to read…" Fiona replied.
"Incentivized. I wouldn't force you to do anything unless it is necessary." Lars clarified.
"Uhm, so in the book that you paid me to read. Why are you a monocle-wearing lunatic that travels the world and kills people?" Fiona asked.

Hearing this, Lars got startled and exclaimed. "What? Why did you pick up the Fall of Martin Orchard? That book is not for children. Your mummy will flip out when she finds out about this."
"Uhm, I didn't want to read one of your children's books. You have already read them to me too many times, so what's the point?" Fiona asked.
"The point is to improve your vocabulary," Lars replied.
"Anyways, why did you describe yourself the way you did?" Fiona asked.
"Because the point of fiction is to create scenarios and see how they play out," Lars replied.
"You mean like 'what if lollies were healthy'?" Fiona asked.
"Well, that's one unlikely scenario, but sure," Lars replied.
"Great, I'll return to my room and ponder on that. See you later," Fiona chirped.

As Fiona returned to her room, she stared at the ceiling in excitement. She wanted to reach the dream world where anything was possible, even healthy lollies. Unfortunately, she couldn't dream on command, as she needed to get sleepy first. 'Hmm, what is the easiest way to fall asleep?' Fiona thought and giggled as she realised the answer. The easiest way was to keep reading her father's book! A few pages later, Fiona reached the world of vivid dreams.

***

'Wow. This is amazing.' Fiona thought as she opened her eyes. She was in a fantasy kingdom where candies were growing on trees and the rivers were flowing with different soft drinks. She crossed a bridge and entered a small Indonesian-inspired village. A signpost mentioned that the village was called Negeri Permen, (Candy Land).

A boy approached her and spoke. "Hi, Fiona. My name is Gula-Gula. I need your help."
Fiona smiled at the boy, who reminded her of her cousin in Indonesia and replied. "I am happy to help. This is my dream, so I can do anything!"
"Can you please ask the fairy Manisan Bonbon to end her curse upon these lands?" Gula-Gula asked. "What curse? Are the candies poisonous?" Fiona asked.
"No, they are nutritious and good for you,"

'Wow. This is amazing.' Fiona thought as she opened her eyes. She was in a fantasy kingdom where candies were growing on trees and the rivers were flowing with different soft drinks.

Gula-Gula replied.
"So, can I eat the lollypops hanging from that tree?" Fiona asked and pointed towards an orange tree that had rainbow flavoured lollypops instead of oranges.
"Yes, they are good for you," Gula-Gula replied.
"Wow!" Fiona exclaimed, rushed to the tree, and grabbed herself a lollypop.

As she licked the lollypop, she felt like she was in heaven. This was the best lollypop she had ever had, and it combined all her favourite flavours. 'I love my imagination!' Fiona thought and smiled.

Fiona's state of blissful gluttony was interrupted when Gula-Gula approached her again. "So, Nona Orchard. Can you please help us now that you tasted our curse?" Her imaginary cousin's statement confused Fiona. What exactly was wrong with this place?

"Uhm Gula-Gula. I don't understand what the problem is. This place seems like paradise." Fiona said. "It only seems that way because it is new to you. Imagine if the only flavour you ever eat is sweet? You would be longing for the vegetables you refuse to eat." Gula-Gula replied.

At first, Fiona stared at the boy in disbelief. Why on Earth would she yearn for veggies when she was eating these yummy lollies?

Fiona had another lick on the lollypop and she understood Gula-Gula's predicament. The appeal of eating solely candies faded quickly, and she yearned for a piece of steamed broccoli.

"Okay. How can I help you?" Fiona asked. "Manisan Bonbon lives on the other side of the forest. I would go myself, but there are werewolves in the forest, and I am too scared." Gula-Gula replied.
"Don't be afraid. I will help you. See you later, cousin." Fiona chirped and used her teleportation abilities to leave the village.

***

'Hmm, this is not the Fairy Castle.' Fiona thought as she opened her eyes in a dark and scary forest. An icy wind hit her, and she shivered from the cold. Yet there was another factor that worried her more. The roaring of an approaching pack of werewolves. Fiona forgot that she was inside a dream and panicked. What would she do?

'If I only had two pistols and a Zetan Monocle like Martin Orchard.' Fiona thought.

Amazement overwhelmed her when the monocle materialised in front of her eyes, and the pistols appeared in her hands.

'Would you like to activate Combat Mode?' The monocle asked Fiona. "Yes, please save me from the nasty werewolves."

Fiona's perception of time slowed down, and she got an out of body experience seeing herself shoot the werewolves in slow motion like an action hero. After a few seconds, Fiona returned to her body and dropped her smoking hot pistols to the ground. She had killed the werewolves.

"No, Fiona. What have you done?"

Fiona turned around and saw an old fairy who held a candy cane. 'That must be Manisan Bonbon the Fairy. I wonder why she is here.' Fiona thought and replied.
"I came to save you from the werewolves."
"Save me? Those werewolves were my friends. Why did you feel compelled to resort to violence, little girl?" Manisan exclaimed.

Fiona thought about Manisan's question. She realised that reading a violent book had impacted her problem-solving abilities. If she had read a peaceful book, she would have come up with a better solution.

"I don't know. They terrified me." 36

Fiona sobbed.

"Your fear is not a reason to harm others. Could you have solved the situation without using violence?" Manisan asked rhetorically.

Fiona put her hands in her pockets, and she felt something crunchy. As she pulled it out, she held a piece of dog treat.

"Yes, I could have given the werewolves the dog treat," Fiona said and sighed.
"Good. Let this be a learning experience. Since this is a dream, your violent outburst had no effect. However, let this be a warning. Giving in to violent thoughts can have irreversible effects." Manisan lectured.
"Yes, Manisan. I am sorry." Fiona replied.
"So, is there anything else?" Manisan asked.
"Uhm, Gula-Gula asked if you can stop the curse that makes all the plants grow candies. He wants to experience other flavours than sweetness." Fiona replied.
"This is your dream, so you can affect anything you want. Your wish is my command," Manisan replied and twirled her magic wand, so stars sparked from it. It was beautiful until a certain voice ended the dream.

***

"I came to save you from the werewolves."
"Save me? Those werewolves were my friends. Why did you feel compelled to resort to violence, little girl?"

She ran to the kitchen, hugged Ling-Ling, and chirped.
"Thank you very much for making me healthy meals mummy. I love you, and I love veggies."

"Fiona. Dinner is ready, honey."

Fiona smiled as she woke up. The dream had taught her to appreciate veggies and it was time to show her appreciation to mummy Ling-Ling.

Hearing this, Ling-Ling gave Lars a sceptical look and said, "What did you do to her?"
"Uhm, I guess I taught her to enjoy vegetables," Lars said in bewilderment.
"Oh well, let's eat," Ling-Ling replied.

Having said this, the family had dinner, and Fiona had an extra-large platter of vegetables to make up for all the candies she ate in her naughty dreams.

The end.

Thanks for reading this book

If you enjoyed reading this anthology of children adventures, please check out my other novels. For more information about my books please visit my website www.Martinlundqvist.com or Google my real name, Martin Lundqvist.

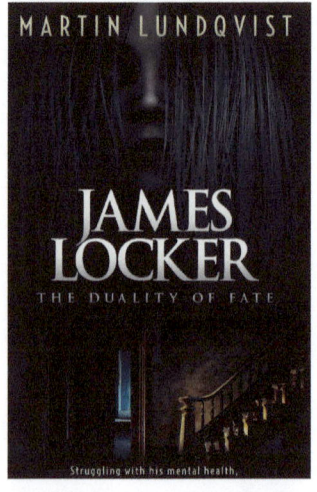

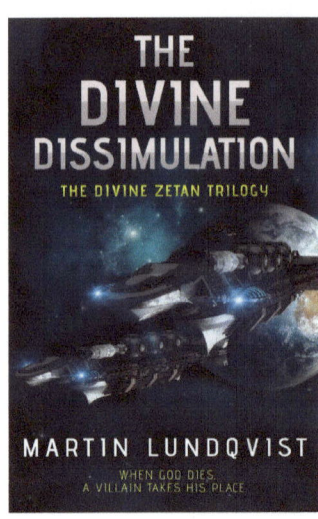

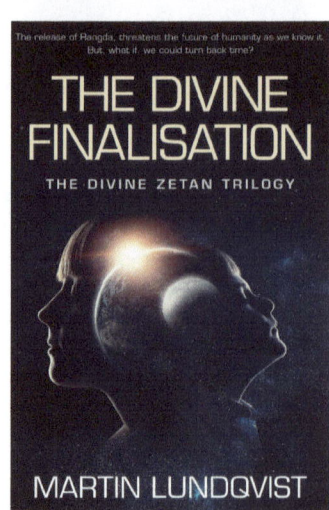
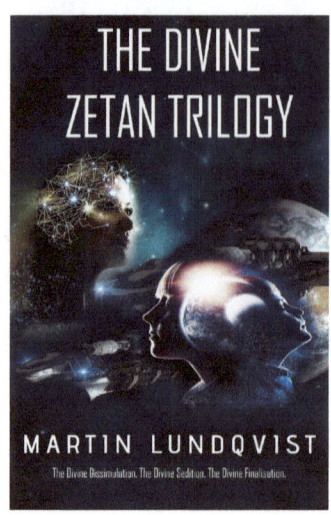

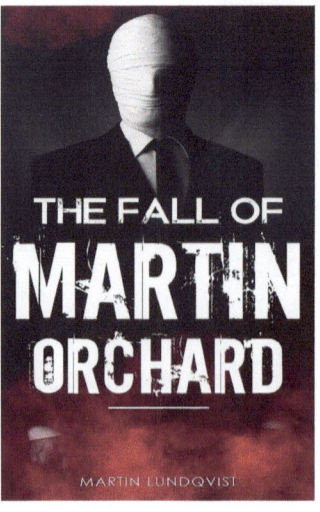
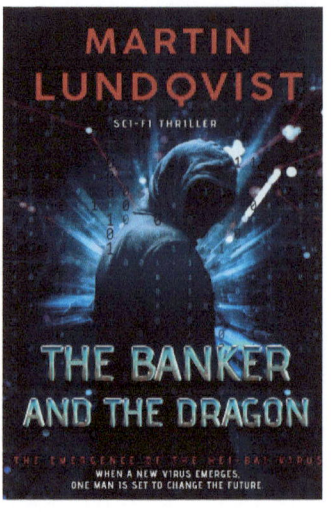